# NATASHA WING'S
# The Night Before
# My First Communion

**Grosset & Dunlap**
An Imprint of Penguin Random House

With special thanks to Kelly Krapes, Deacon Don Weiss,
and Teresa, Roger, and Ava Funke—NW

To Father George—faithful priest, devoted teacher,
loving uncle . . . and inspiration to us all—AW

GROSSET & DUNLAP
Penguin Young Readers Group
An Imprint of Penguin Random House LLC

Text copyright © 2018 by Natasha Wing. Illustrations copyright © 2018 by Penguin Random House LLC. All rights reserved.
Published by Grosset & Dunlap, an imprint of Penguin Random House LLC, 345 Hudson Street, New York, New York 10014.
GROSSET & DUNLAP is a trademark of Penguin Random House LLC. Manufactured in China.

Library of Congress Cataloging-in-Publication Data is available.

ISBN 9781524786199                    10 9 8

# NATASHA WING'S
# The Night Before
# My First Communion

## By Natasha Wing
## Illustrated by Amy Wummer

Grosset & Dunlap
An Imprint of Penguin Random House

'Twas the night before Communion,
our very first one.
We had studied so hard
and now we were done.

Our outfits were hung
in the closet with care.

Mom set out a tie
for my brother to wear.

Our grandparents arrived.
Our cousins came, too.

"We're so excited," said Grandma,
"to share this with you."

Sun streamed through stained glass,
casting colors everywhere.

I cupped my hands,
but they shook even more.
What if I drop
the Host on the floor?

At church we rehearsed walking in a straight line,

then practiced receiving
the bread and the wine.

We both want to make
our family so proud.
But what if I trip
or Max sneezes out loud?

"It'll be a great day," the priest told our class.
"Go get some sleep, and I'll see you at Mass."

That night we nestled all snug in our beds,
while visions of angels danced in our heads.

In the morning that Sunday I put on my dress.
"You look so grown up!" said my big cousin Tess.

Then my brother appeared in his tie and his suit.
Mom hugged him and said, "Aww, don't you look cute!"

Dad took lots of photos
of my brother and me.
Everyone in our family
was as proud as could be.

On the way to church,
I stayed calm—well, I tried.

But once Mass began,
I grew nervous inside.

It seemed like forever
before the priest raised the cup.

After he blessed the offerings, it was my turn to go up!

I walked down the aisle
with hands folded in prayer.

Then, looking around,
what did my wondering eyes see
but the gentle Lord Jesus
looking down upon me.

His eyes almost seemed
to gaze into mine.
And I knew right then,
it all would be fine.

When Mass was over,
we took pictures with the priest.

At last it was time
for the Communion Day feast!
The party was so fun!
It was like a reunion.
We ate and celebrated
our First Holy Communion.

We opened our presents—
Rosary beads! Photo frames!

Our cousins gave us Bibles
embossed with our names.

My godmother, Rosa,
took me aside.
She gave me a box
with a necklace inside.

Much later, at bedtime,
Mom tucked us in tight.
"Happy First Communion to you.
God bless and good night."